MR. SUN
AND MR. SEA

AN AFRICAN LEGEND RETOLD BY
ANDREA BUTLER
ILLUSTRATED BY LILY TOY HONG

📚 GoodYearBooks

Long, long ago, Mr. Sun lived by Mr. Sea.

Mr. Sun went to visit Mr. Sea every
day. But Mr. Sea never, ever went to
visit Mr. Sun.

One day, Mr. Sun asked, "Why don't you visit me?"

"I have too many children,"
said Mr. Sea.

"My house is very big,"
said Mr. Sun. "I can fit all of
you in my house. Please come."

The next day, Mr. Sea and his children knocked at Mr. Sun's door.

"May we come in?" asked Mr. Sea.
"Yes, yes," said Mr. Sun.

Mr. Sun opened the door.
In came the starfish, the crayfish,
and some sea water.

The water came up to Mr. Sun's knees.
It got higher and higher.

In came the big fish, the little fish, and more sea water.

The water came up to Mr. Sun's chest.
It got higher and higher.

In came the crabs, the seaweed, and more sea water.

The water came up to Mr. Sun's neck.
It got higher and higher.

Mr. Sun jumped up on the roof.
Soon the water came over the roof.

15

So Mr. Sun jumped up, up, up into the sky and never, ever came down. There he stays to this very day.